W9-BGP-552

CUENTO DE LUZ

The most moving moments of our lives find us without words.
We connect with nature in silence.
When the eagle flies over us and the wolf howls, everything is said.

— Ana Eulate & Nívola Uyá —

Walking Eagle: The Little Comanche Boy

Text © Ana Eulate
Illustrations © Nívola Uyá
This edition © 2013 Cuento de Luz SL
Calle Claveles 10 | Urb Monteclaro | Pozuelo de Alarcón | 28223 | Madrid | Spain
www.cuentodeluz.com
Title in Spanish: Águila que Camina: El niño comanche
English translation by Jon Brokenbrow

ISBN: 978-84-15784-36-4

Printed by Shanghai Chenxi Printing Co., Ltd. July 2013, print number 1381-4

Walking Eagle

The Little Comanche Boy

Ana Eulate ★ Nívola Uyá

Walking Eagle rode along the path.

They were waiting for him, like they did every evening.

He told stories, tales told without words.

Because Walking Eagle didn't speak,

he used his hands, his face, his smile and his eyes

to communicate everything that his listeners needed to hear.

Walking Eagle was born clubfooted.

As soon as he could stand, when he was very small,
he looked down and saw his feet pointing inwards,
and that his legs made the shape of
a heart.

He belonged to the **Comanche tribe,**
called the Lords of the Plains,
originally from the Rocky Mountains.
But he also belonged to nature.

Walking Eagle merged with the trees, disappeared into the **forests.**

The **animals would approach him,** and he fearlessly looked them in the eyes,

hugged them and gave them names, and fed them.

Born to ride,
the little Comanche boy
had legs in the shape of a heart
to bond to his kindred spirit:
his Pinto horse, on whose back
he would fly, galloping into the air,
taking his stories with him.

He walked down a path
of red earth.

A path that ran alongside a river. A river that ran around a range of mountains.

Walking Eagle wore his feather headdress.
After listening to his tales, each different tribe
would solemnly give him
a feather
from a majestic eagle
as a gift,

as a present,

as an offering

for the legacy

they had received.

And all of these feathers
from his different "brothers,"
as Walking Eagle liked to call them,
formed this special headdress,

the one that crowned his head and accompanied his tales.

Before reaching the place where they waited for him, to listen to his tale,

Walking Eagle sat down on his makeshift chair made of dry leaves and clay

mixed with different **memories**.

There he would close his eyes,
relax, dream, and ...

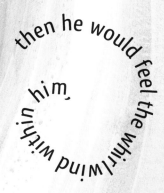

then he would feel the whirlwind within him,

a very powerful emotion,
goose bumps,
the rhythm of his heart as he galloped.

He heard laughter, enveloped in the perfume of flowers,
and the voice of a woman with sparkling eyes
who called to him:

Waaaalllkiiing Eeeeaaglllle!!!!

They were memories of *his* mother that sometimes came to him on the wind.

That whirlwind, that voice, that perfume—

Yes! That was it!

It was what inspired him to continue on his way,

with just his horse and his stories,

crossing territories,

struggling to make

different peoples

hold hands

and listen to what he had to say.

Walking Eagle, the little Comanche boy

who took tales to different tribes,

spoke of **togetherness,**

solidarity,

joining hands,

and overcoming fears.

Through his vivid performances,

he inspired his listeners with stories

of warriors who laid down their spears,

and impressed them by silently imitating

the howling of wolves, the flapping

of wings on the earth and in the air,

and majestic eagles who watch over us

and guide us on our way.

His animated gestures
cast larger-than-life shadows
in the heat of the fire.

With his hands, Walking Eagle made it possible to feel **the light** of the full moon,

the caress of the wind, the crackling of the flames.

A bright, white magical thread would appear
while Walking Eagle told his tales with his hands,
bringing together territories, countries and continents.

Then the magical thread
wove an **ENORMOUS TEEPEE**
where they all could meet around the warmth of the fire.

And it was there,

to the sound of drumming

and chanting in the moonlight,

that all of the Native American tribes

encouraged people of different colored skins

from around the world to come together as one

by linking their fingers and hearts in solidarity.

The little boy with the feather headdress
and legs in the shape of a heart
continued along the path.
They were waiting for him.
He told tales.

Tales that were told **without words** ...